CLEAN HOUSE

CLEAN HOUSE

by Jessie Haas
pictures by Yossi Abolafia

GREENWILLOW BOOKS NEW YORK

Printed in the United States of America
First Edition   10 9 8 7 6 5 4 3 2 1

✦ ✦ ✦

Library of Congress Cataloging-in-Publication Data
Haas, Jessie.
Clean house / by Jessie Haas ; pictures by Yossi
Abolafia.
    p.   cm.
Summary: After Mom and Tess thoroughly clean
house in preparation for a visit from Aunt Alice
and Cousin Kate, both mothers and daughters
admit that they prefer a "normal" mess.
ISBN 0-688-14079-3
[1. Mothers and daughters—Fiction.
2. House cleaning—Fiction.]   I. Abolafia, Yossi, ill.
II. Title.   PZ7.H1129Cl   1996   [E]—dc20
95-973   CIP   AC

For Bernard and Molly,
who have been known to do this

— J. H.

For Rami

—Y. A.

CHAPTER ONE

Mom and Tess were eating supper when the phone rang.

"You are?" Mom said.

"Yes, do!" she said.

"When?" she said. "Oh, no, that would be fine."

"Aunt Alice and Cousin Kate are coming to visit!" Mom said when she hung up.

"Hurray!" yelled Tess. Kate was the cousin she'd liked best last year at the big family picnic.

"It will be nice," said Mom. "But, Tess, they're coming in just three days! How will we get this house clean?"

Tess looked around. "What's wrong with this house?"

"There's a cat on the table, for one thing!" said Mom.

"Milkshake always sits there," said Tess. "He's waiting for my leftovers."

"There are books on all the chairs," said Mom.

"Right where we can get one when we want it," said Tess.

"And Ranger has chewed this potholder," said Mom. "And, Tess, your sneakers are all over the floor!"

"There are only two of them," Tess said. "How can two sneakers be all over the floor?"

"One is over *there*," said Mom, "and one is over *here*. And that's just the kitchen."

"Kate won't care," said Tess. "And neither will Aunt Alice."

"I'm not so sure," said Mom. "When I visited their house last year, it was spotless. Quick, Tess, finish your dinner. We have to start cleaning right away."

After supper Tess put her sneakers in the hall closet. Mom peeked inside it. "Oh, *look* at that mess!"

"We'll keep the door closed," said Tess.

"We'll have to open it sometime," Mom said. She pulled things out of the bottom of the closet. Deck shoes. A fishing basket. Ballet shoes. Half a pair of galoshes. The boots Tess wore when she was a baby. The boots she wore when she was three. The boots she wore when she was five.

"Now it's a *worse* mess," said Tess.

"Get a garbage bag," said Mom. "We'll give things away to the Red Cross."

Ranger came and sniffed the pile. He picked up something and carried it away to his corner.

Mom and Tess filled two garbage bags with boots and old coats. Mom hung up the fishing pole and the fishing basket in the back of the closet. She vacuumed the closet floor.

Then Tess tried to put her sneakers away again. She could find only one.

"Mom," Tess said, "we gave my sneaker away!"

"I'll find it," Mom said. She put her head in one bag. She hunted and hunted.

Tess dumped the other bag onto the floor again. She picked up every boot and every shoe.

"Mom, it's not here!"

Mom pulled her head out of the bag. She

looked across the kitchen. "Oh, Ranger, bad dog!" she said. Ranger was chewing Tess's sneaker. Now it looked like a sandal.

"You'll have to wear your good shoes tomorrow," Mom said. She tied up the garbage bags and carried them out to the garage.

"Bedtime," she said to Tess. "And we hardly got anything done!"

"I put one of my sneakers away," said Tess.

CHAPTER TWO

Mom woke Tess up early in the morning.
"We'll try to do a little cleaning before we leave,"
she said.

"What about breakfast?" asked Tess.

"Bring it up here," said Mom. "You can eat
while you clean your room."

Tess put her cereal and orange juice on her bedside table. She picked up three shirts, and she put them on the laundry pile. She ate a bite of cereal. She hung one skirt in her closet.

When Tess turned around, Milkshake was drinking from her cereal bowl.

"Milkshake!" yelled Tess. Milkshake jumped off the table. The cereal bowl landed upside down on Tess's pillow. The orange juice splashed on the wall.

Mom came to the door. "This isn't working," she said.

Mom put the pillow in the washing machine. Tess wiped the orange juice off the wall. Then they both sat down to breakfast.

"Come straight home from school," said Mom. "I'll get out of work early, and we'll clean some more. Now go find your shoes. Then you can help me wash these dishes. We left the supper dishes last night, too."

But Tess's shoes weren't in the corner where she thought they were. They weren't under the

bed—but a lot of other things were! They weren't in the closet—but she did find two lost library books.

"Mom!" yelled Tess.

Mom came to help look. But Ranger found Tess's good shoes first.

"I can't wear one shoe and one sneaker!" Tess said.

"We'll stop at the store on the way to school and get you a pair of sneakers," said Mom. "Oh, dear! Now there are supper dishes *and* breakfast dishes to do!"

CHAPTER THREE

Mom and Tess got home early.

"You vacuum the living room," Mom said. "I'll mop the kitchen."

Tess got the vacuum cleaner out of the closet and plugged it in. It was a loud vacuum cleaner, but Tess liked it because it had a headlight.

Tess pretended the vacuum cleaner was a truck. *Vroom, vroom, vroom-oom!*

She was turning the big truck around in a tiny parking lot. She had to do it without squashing anyone. *Vroom—oops!* The vacuum cleaner started to swallow Milkshake's catnip mouse. Tess put the mouse on the coffee table.

Vroom, vroo—sppppp! The vacuum cleaner tried to suck up a piece of Tess's homework. Tess put the homework on the coffee table. *Vroom!*

Milkshake ran in from the kitchen. He jumped onto the coffee table. He made four wet tracks on Tess's homework. He shook his paws. Milkshake didn't like mopping.

Vroom, vroom. The vacuum sucked up one of Tess's hair ties. *Vroo-oo-ooom*, it got a tiny doll dress.

"Sorry, ma'am," said Tess. "It's hard to turn this truck around—oops!"

Now the vacuum was swallowing one of Milkshake's toys. It was just a piece of string, but it was the *best* piece.

Tess tried to turn off the vacuum. Too late! The string was gone.

"Don't worry, Milkshake," said Tess. "I'll get it back."

Tess opened the vacuum cleaner. She took out the bag, and she looked through the little hole. She couldn't see Milkshake's toy at all.

"It has to be in there," said Tess. She got a crochet hook from Mom's basket. She stuck it inside the hole, and she pulled. Out came a lot of dust.

She pulled again. Out came her hair tie, and some more dust. Next came the doll dress, covered with carpet fluff. Then a rubber band, and two candy wrappers, and a *lot* more dust.

"Don't worry, Milkshake," Tess said. She pushed the crochet hook way inside the bag. She wiggled it. She pulled. Out came more dust. With the dust was one end of Milkshake's toy.

"I've got it!" yelled Tess. She pulled.

Milkshake saw his string. He jumped for it. *Bang!* went the coffee table. *Whumpf!* Milkshake landed on the vacuum bag. A cloud of dust came puffing out the hole. Tess coughed and wiped her eyes.

Ranger was barking to be let in.

"Tess!" called Mom. "Let him in the front door, so he doesn't get tracks on my clean floor!"

Tess opened the front door. Her fingers made smudges on the knob.

Ranger saw Milkshake playing with the string. He wanted to play, too. He jumped at Milkshake. He picked up the vacuum cleaner bag.

"No!" yelled Tess.

Ranger shook the bag. Dust flew everywhere. Tess tried to take the bag. Ranger ran away from her. He ran straight to the kitchen. He shook the bag again. It split open, right in the middle of the clean, wet floor.

Mom didn't say anything. She looked at
Ranger. She looked at Milkshake. She looked at
Tess. Then she sat down on a chair, and she closed
her eyes.

"All right," she said finally. "Let's try again. Tess,
you vacuum. I'll mop. But, first, we're going to
lock Ranger and Milkshake in the bathroom."

CHAPTER FOUR

Mom mopped. Tess vacuumed.

Then they cleaned up the bathroom. Milkshake had made tracks in the tub. Ranger had chewed the bath mat.

Mom vacuumed. Tess wiped up the cat tracks.

Then they started to clean the rest of the house.

Mom gathered up all her books with people kissing on the covers. She piled them in the bottom of her closet. Only her big fat schoolbooks stayed out.

Tess took her cat and castle drawings off the refrigerator door.

"Don't throw those away!" said Mom. She put the drawings in her special box under the bed.

Mom took the picture of herself in her new bathing suit off the refrigerator door.

"Don't throw that away!" said Tess. She took the picture upstairs, and she pinned it to her lampshade.

Mom cleaned the inside of the refrigerator, too. She threw away leftovers. She threw away the grape jelly that they both hated, that Grandma gave them every year. She threw away the mold Tess was growing for science class.

"You can start some more after they leave," she told Tess.

Mom washed the windows. First she washed them inside, and then she washed them outside.

When Mom washed outside, Milkshake sat inside on the sill. He pressed his nose on the glass to watch Mom. Every place Milkshake pressed his nose, he left a little smudge on the clean glass. When Mom came inside, she could see the smudges easily because the glass was so clean.

Tess cleaned her room. She put her dolls
and her trucks, her model horses, her top
and her jacks and her Chinese checkers in a
great big box. Then she dragged the box into
her closet. The box looked very messy. But
her room looked empty and clean.

Mom tripped over the vacuum. She said it didn't hurt much.

Tess broke two fingernails trying to open the toilet cleaner. That hurt a lot!

"Isn't it clean *enough?*" Tess asked while Mom helped her put on Band-Aids.

Mom looked around. "Oh, Tess," she said, "Aunt Alice's table was so polished I could see my face in it. You could have eaten off her kitchen floor. We can't give up now."

Mom vacuumed the whole upstairs. Then she got out the throw rugs she'd bought last year on sale. She put one in the downstairs hall and one in the upstairs hall.

"They look pretty," Tess said. "Why don't we use them all the time?"

"Because they'll get dirty," Mom said. "They're just for company."

Out in the kitchen something clattered.
Milkshake came racing around the corner, with
Ranger after him. Milkshake skidded on the rug
and scrunched it into the corner of the hall. He hit
the table with the lamp on it. So did Ranger. The
lamp fell on top of them.

"*Myreow!*" said Milkshake. He raced upstairs.

Swoosh! went the upstairs throw rug. *Crash!* went something else.

"*Yarf!*" said Ranger. He raced into the living room.

Bang! went the coffee table.

Mom sat down on the bottom of the stairs. She held her head in her hands.

"Now we know why they call them throw rugs," said Tess.

After supper Mom and Tess were too tired to wash dishes. After breakfast there were too many, and they didn't have time. The next time supper came around, they went out for pizza.

"But we'll have to wash dishes when we get home," Mom said. "They're coming tomorrow!"

Mom washed. Tess dried. It got later and later and later.

When all the dishes were washed, Mom and Tess looked around. Everything was clean. Everything was shiny. There were no books on the table. There were no books on the chairs or the stairs, in the bathroom, or on the coffee table. There was nothing to trip on in the hall. There were only two smudges on the window, and Mom wiped them off.

"Doesn't the house look *nice!*" Mom said.

"I guess so," Tess said. The house did seem bigger, and it seemed emptier. It seemed quiet, and it seemed restful.

"Let's *keep* it this way," Mom said. "Then we'll never have to work this hard, ever again."

But there was something Tess didn't like about the house. She tried to think what it was, and right in the middle she gave a big yawn.

Time for bed!

CHAPTER FIVE

The next morning Mom and Tess were careful.

Tess ate dry cereal straight from the box, so she wouldn't get a bowl dirty. She played with Ranger in the backyard, so neither of them messed anything up.

Mom washed her teacup as soon as she was finished. Then she put it away on a shelf. She read the newspaper outside on the deck. When she was done, she threw it in the recycling bin.

Kate and Aunt Alice came at lunchtime.

When Kate got out of the car, Tess saw that she was taller. She smiled at Tess, but it was a small, shy smile, not like the big grin Tess remembered from the picnic.

Aunt Alice looked tired from her long drive. But her clothes looked nice, and every hair was in place. You could have eaten off the floor of her car. Now Tess believed that Aunt Alice's house was spotless.

"Come in," said Mom. She hugged Aunt Alice lightly, so she didn't wrinkle Aunt Alice's blouse. "I'll fix some lunch."

Mom made sandwiches and put them on plates. She cut each sandwich in half, from corner to corner. She poured the milk into a pitcher, and at the table she poured it all out again into their glasses.

Kate and Aunt Alice sat straight in their chairs.

"What a nice house," Aunt Alice said, looking around. "So clean and neat."

Kate didn't say anything. She sat up straight, and crossed her legs, and ate one triangle of her sandwich.

Milkshake jumped up beside Kate's plate.
For a second Kate almost smiled.

"Bad cat!" Mom said. She picked up
Milkshake and dumped him outside.

Kate stopped smiling. Mom and Aunt Alice
talked about the weather.

After lunch Mom showed Kate and Aunt Alice their room.

"You probably want to rest after your long drive," she said. "Tess and I will just wash up the dishes."

"Oh. All right," said Aunt Alice. Kate didn't say anything.

Mom and Tess washed the four plates and the four glasses and the pitcher. Mom wiped the table. Tess looked around the kitchen. There wasn't a crumb left in sight.

"Why the big sigh?" Mom asked.

"Kate doesn't seem as much fun as last year," said Tess.

"She's probably just tired," said Mom. "Give her time."

"I'm tired, too," Tess said. "I guess I'll take a nap."

Tess went upstairs. She lay on her neatly made

bed. She looked around. Every book was on its shelf. Every toy was hidden away in the big box in Tess's closet. "Hmph!" Tess said. She closed her eyes.

CHAPTER SIX

In the next room Tess heard bedsprings jounce.

"Mom?" Kate said. "Do we have to stay here all weekend?"

Tess opened her eyes wide. What did Kate mean?

"Yes," said Aunt Alice. "What's the problem?"

"It's boring," Kate said. "There aren't any books, and there aren't any toys, and they won't let the animals in . . . and Tess doesn't seem as much fun as last year."

Tess sat up straight on her bed. Her face felt hot. Hey! she thought.

"Some people do keep neat houses," Aunt Alice said. "Not everybody is like us."

But Aunt Alice's house was spotless! Mom said so!

"Remember how hard we cleaned, when Tess's mom came last year?" Aunt Alice asked.

After a minute Kate laughed. "Remember when you tripped on the mop pail when you went to answer the phone? And it was the wrong number?"

"Remember how tired we were?" Aunt Alice asked. "And remember we said from now on we'd *keep* our house clean, so we wouldn't have to work so hard ever again?"

Now Kate and Aunt Alice both laughed.

Hey! thought Tess. *Hey!* Now she understood everything.

Tess got up from her bed and went softly downstairs. Mom was napping in her rocking chair in the spotless living room. Milkshake sat outside on the window ledge. He pressed his nose to the glass and meowed. Ranger whined outside the back door.

Tess opened the back door and let Ranger in. She opened the front door and let Milkshake in. Then she went into the living room. She got Milkshake's best string out of his basket. She wiggled it on the floor, where Milkshake could see it.

Milkshake pounced on the string.

Ranger wanted to play, too. He jumped after Milkshake.

Milkshake raced into the downstairs hall. The throw rug slid. *Crash!* went the lamp. *Bang!* went the coffee table. *Swoosh* went the upstairs throw rug, and *tinkle* went something else.

"Oh, my goodness!" Mom said in her rocking chair. "What on earth is happening?"

Kate and Aunt Alice came to the door of their room. "Is anyone hurt?" Aunt Alice asked.

Kate was starting to smile.

Tess ran past them into her room. She opened her closet door. She grabbed the edge of her big box, and she pulled.

The box tipped over. *Crash! Rumble!* Out spilled the dolls and the trucks, the model horses, the top and the jacks and the Chinese checkers.

"Hey, Kate!" yelled Tess. Her voice sounded strange in the quiet house. So Tess yelled louder. *"Hey, Kate!* Let's play! What do you like best?"

Kate came to the door of Tess's room. She grinned the big grin that Tess remembered from the picnic.

"I like *everything!*" Kate said. "Let's play with everything at once!"

When Tess and Kate were hungry, they came downstairs. Mom and Aunt Alice were in the living room, talking and laughing. They both had their feet on the coffee table. Aunt Alice was playing string toy with Milkshake. Ranger was in the corner, chewing his potholder.

"Hey, Tess," Mom said. "Grab that bag of corn chips, please? And the jar of salsa?"

"You want the salsa in a bowl?" Tess asked. "And the corn chips on a plate?"

Mom looked at Aunt Alice. They both laughed.

"No, Tess," Mom said. "The normal way is just fine!"